D1058371

TIME HOP SWEETS SHOP
Ice Cream with
Albert Einstein

By Reese Everett

Illustrated by Sally Garland

ST. JOHN THE BAPTIST PARISH LIBRARY
2920 NEW HIGHWAY 51
LAPLACE, LOUISIANA 70068

Rourke
Educational Media
rourkeeducationalmedia.com

© 2016 Rourke Educational Media

All rights reserved. No part of this book may be reproduced or utilized in any form or by any means, electronic or mechanical including photocopying, recording, or by any information storage and retrieval system without permission in writing from the publisher.

www.rourkeeducationalmedia.com

Edited by: Keli Sipperley
Cover and Interior layout by: Tara Raymo
Cover and Interior Illustrations by: Sally Garland

Library of Congress PCN Data

Ice Cream with Albert Einstein / Reese Everett
(Time Hop Sweets Shop)
ISBN (hard cover)(alk. paper) 978-1-68191-376-6
ISBN (soft cover) 978-1-68191-418-3
ISBN (e-Book) 978-1-68191-459-6
Library of Congress Control Number: 2015951489

Printed in the United States of America,
North Mankato, Minnesota

Dear Parents and Teachers,

Fiona and Finley are just like any modern-day kids. They help out with the family business, face struggles and triumphs at school, travel through time with important historical figures ...

Well, maybe that part's not so ordinary. At the Time Hop Sweets Shop, anything can happen, at any point in time. The family bakery draws customers from all over the map—and all over the history books. And when Tick Tock the parrot squawks, Fiona and Finley know an adventure is about to begin!

These beginner chapter books are designed to introduce students to important people in U.S. history, turning their accomplishments into adventures that Fiona, Finley, and young readers get to experience right along with them.

Perfect as read-alouds, read-alongs, or independent readers, books in the Time Hop Sweets Shop series were written to delight, inform, and engage your child or students by making each historical figure memorable and relatable. Each book includes a biography, comprehension questions, websites for further reading, and more.

We look forward to our time travels together!

Happy Reading,
Rourke Educational Media

Table of Contents

Freezing Time

Finley stared at the container oozing brown goo on the counter. He wrinkled his forehead. He scrunched his nose. He wiggled his eyebrows. Then he sneezed.

"Squawk! Bless You! Squawk!" Tick Tock, the family parrot, screeched.

"Thanks, Tock," Finley said. He sighed and wiggled his fingers at the goo.

Fiona, his younger sister, burst through the door as Finley muttered under his breath. "What in the world are you doing?" she asked.

Finley looked up quickly before looking back down at the container. Then he looked at his sister again.

"What in the world are you WEARING?"

Finley licked some goo off his finger and walked around the counter to get a closer look at his sister.

"They're solar eclipse glasses!" Fiona said, flipping her curly red hair off her shoulder and striking a pose. "We got some for you, too!"

"Sweet," Finley said, slipping his on. "These are awesome!"

Fiona pointed to the mess. "Really, what are you doing? Does Mom know you're back here? She has at least a billion customers out there. She—"

"She knows," Finley interrupted. "I'm working on a new recipe. It's ice cream that never melts! Except the only problem is, it does melt. It melts a lot. Just like regular ice cream." Finley wiggled his fingers toward the container again.

Fiona giggled. "Are you trying to put a spell on it?"

"Yep," Finley said. "Nothing else is working so I thought magic was worth a shot."

"But you're not a magician," Fiona said. She stuck her finger in the goo and tasted it. "Yum. It does taste good, though."

Finley nodded. He was sort of a magician in the kitchen. He didn't earn the Cupcake King title for nothing, after all. But he didn't know how to cast spells or do any kind of real magic. And magic was the only ingredient he could think of to keep his ice cream from melting.

The family hiking trip would start the next day in the Old Town Mountains. They planned to watch a solar eclipse from the mountain's summit on the third day. Finley wanted to pack ice cream to celebrate reaching the peak.

"Fiona! Finley!" Dad called from the front of the shop. "Come out here!" His voice sounded excited. Their father's voice was always excited, like something great was about to happen any second. They liked that about him.

A Bright Idea

They raced through the swinging doors and tumbled out into the Sweets Shop. Dad was holding something shiny, showing it off to a customer. Finley clutched his ice cream, still wearing his solar eclipse glasses, and still hoping to make some magic happen.

"What is it?" Fiona asked, hopping up and down, trying to get a better look.

"It's my compass I used at camp when I was a kid," Dad said, handing it to Fiona.

"Wowza!" Fiona exclaimed. "It's so OLD! Just like you, Dad!"

"Hey!" Dad laughed. "I'm not that old!"

"Look at the time! Look at the time!" Tick Tock squawked. The family looked at the shop's side door. Tick Tock always knew when someone special was about to come in. It opened slowly, the bell above it tinkling.

"What, may I ask, are those marvelous things on your faces?" The man who walked in asked, looking at the kids with a fascinated expression. Shocks of white hair sprung from every direction, and he spoke with an accent they didn't recognize.

"They're solar eclipse glasses," Fiona said, striking a pose again. "Aren't they cool?"

"Cool," the man repeated. "Yes, I'd say so."

"Nice to see you again, Albert," Mom said. She reached across the counter and gave his hand a squeeze.

Finley fiddled with his hearing aids. "Did she just say Albert? And again?" He peered at the man through squinted eyes. "Are you EINSTEIN?" he screeched, his voice catching in his throat like a lump just appeared there.

Finley read about Albert Einstein at school. He was one of the world's all-time most famous scientists! And Mom KNEW him? She has a lot of explaining to do, Finley thought.

The man chuckled and pushed his glasses up on his nose. "I am. You can call me Albert, though. And you must be Finley." He nodded toward Fiona. "And you must be Fiona. I've heard a lot about you both."

"You have? How? How do you know Mom?" Fiona couldn't get her words out fast enough.

"Well," Albert said, "I guess you could say she's a chip off the old block." He smiled slyly. Fiona and Finley looked at each other, confusion all over their faces.

"Ahh," he said, pointing to the compass in Fiona's hand. "That brings back memories. A compass started everything for me."

"Did it point you in the right direction?" Finley joked.

Albert laughed. "Sort of. My father gave one to me to play with when I was about five. I was fascinated by it." He reached out his hand. "May I?" he asked.

Fiona handed him the compass. Albert held it up, turning it this way and that.

"See? No matter which way you turn it, the needle always points toward the north. I wanted to know why. That experience made a deep and lasting impression on me," he said. "Something deeper had to be hidden behind things."

Albert handed the compass back to Fiona, then looked at Finley. "For example, there must be something deeper hidden in the reason you're clutching that ice cream."

Finley looked down. Ice cream dripped from the container, sliding down his hands, trickling on the floor.

"Oops," he said, blushing at the mess he'd made. "I'm trying to invent a recipe that will keep it from melting. I'm not having any luck."

"Luck is relative," Albert said. "Just like time. Maybe you just need more of it."

"Luck?" Finley asked, his brows furrowed.

"Time," Albert laughed. "Or perhaps a way to send frozen ice cream to the exact time you want to eat it." He raised his eyebrows and winked.

Finley's face lit up. "Can I do that?"

"Maybe. But your glasses gave me another idea. Do you have a pair I can borrow? I've always wanted to see for myself the eclipse that proved my theory of relativity correct."

"That's what made you famous!" Finley exclaimed. "Can we come too?"

"Yes, yes, yes! Please?" Fiona pleaded.

"Of course," Albert said.

"Be back in time for our trip," Dad said. "And don't lose that compass!"

Albert clutched their hands as they walked out of the Sweets Shop's side door. "To May 29, 1919, on the island of Principe we go," he said. "Hold onto your glasses!"

Family Secrets

Everything whooshed and whirled, whirled and whooshed. Then they were in a clearing near a forest. A man stood surrounded by telescopes, mirrors and other important-looking devices.

"Who is that?"

"He's an astronomer. We shouldn't disturb him. His work in these moments will capture the proof needed to demonstrate my theory," Albert whispered. "And don't look at the sun without those glasses on. It will damage your eyes."

"I can't even see the sun, it's so cloudy," Fiona said, frowning.

"What is he doing?" Finley asked. "And just how does your theory of relativity work, anyway?"

"Well, the theory has two parts, special relativity and general relativity. Special relativity says that it is impossible to know if you are moving unless you can see another object. General relativity says that it is impossible to tell the difference between gravity and the force of **inertia** from a moving object. Gravity is a property of the geometry of space and time, or space-time. Huge objects cause a distortion in space-time, which is felt as gravity."

Finley fiddled with his hearing aids. Fiona wrinkled her nose.

"Huh?" they both said.

"Each time you measure how someone or something experiences time, it's always in relation to something else," Albert said. "What you measure for length, time, and **mass** depends on your own motion relative to your frame of reference. And everything is in motion. Even though you feel like you are standing still, you are actually spinning, because the Earth itself is spinning on its axis. And not only that, the Earth is also orbiting around the sun. We're on a constant ride!"

The thought made Finley dizzy.

ST. JOHN THE BAPTIST PARISH LIBRARY
2920 NEW HIGHWAY 51
LAPLACE, LOUISIANA 70068

"But the speed of light stays the same, no matter how fast or slow you're going," Albert continued. "And nothing can move faster than light. Whether someone is here on Earth or in the farthest corner of the universe, we all obey the same laws of light and gravity," he said. "But though we all follow these laws, we still experience time and the universe in different ways. What for us might be a million years may be just seconds for someone traveling at light speed in a rocket ship."

Finley and Fiona thought about this for a moment.

"So does that mean if it only takes me a short time to travel at the speed of light to a faraway planet, in that time, hundreds of years could pass on Earth?"

"Exactly!" Albert clapped his hands together. "If you move quickly enough, what you observe about space and time will be different from what other people who are moving at different speeds will observe."

"Weird," Fiona said.

Finley watched the astronomer in the distance. He paced back and forth, looking at the sky. Clouds loomed overhead. He'd never seen an eclipse before, but Finley imagined the clouds might be a problem.

"So what does the eclipse have to do with your theory, anyway?" he asked.

"Well, when those clouds clear, that man will take a photograph. It will show that the sun's gravity changes the path of light from stars that surround it. When he compares the photo to photos of the same stars in the night sky, he will see the stars in different locations, proving my general theory. This is because a gravitational field is really a curving of space, which is inseparable from time."

"Whoa," Finley said.

"Wowza," Fiona said.

"Cool, huh?" Albert said.

"It's making me dizzy to think about it," Finley admitted.

"Does your theory explain how we can go back in time from the Sweets Shop?" Fiona asked.

Albert winked at her, and pointed to the sky. The clouds shifted. The moon stood stark and dark, blocking out the sun. The astronomer busied himself with his equipment, taking photos and making calculations that would soon make Albert a celebrity all over the world.

"It's beautiful," Fiona whispered.

"Amazing," Finley agreed.

"I wish we had some of that ice cream," Albert said.

"We could go back to the future and get some," Finley said.

"We could, though we would be returning to your present, not the future," Albert explained.

"But it's the future for you," Fiona said. "Right?"

"It is," Albert said.

"So how does our Sweets Shop work, Albert? Do you know? Why can we get customers from any point in history, but never from the future?" Finley asked.

"How do you know you haven't had visitors from the future?" Albert replied. "You may not have recognized them from your history books, but that doesn't mean everyone who comes in the door is from the present or the past."

Fiona and Finley looked at each other. "WOWZA!"

"Your mother knows a thing or two about that. My great-great niece was always up for an adventure with visitors from her own future, as well as her past." Albert grinned.

"Wait, does that mean, you're our great-great-great uncle?" Fiona exclaimed.

"That would make you a really great uncle!" Finley said.

"I have another secret for you," Albert said. "Take a closer look at that compass. Do you see anything unusual?"

Fiona and Finley stared at the compass. They didn't see anything strange.

"Think about where you want to go in time, then look again," Albert said.

A bright blue arrow appeared on the compass, pointing toward the east.

"It's pointing you to the closest time hop portal," Einstein said.

"Wowza!" Fiona said.

"Double wowza!" Finley said. "Does Dad know about this?"

"You'll have to ask him," Albert said, smiling. "Shall we return? You have a camping trip to get ready for."

"Can we use the compass to send the ice cream forward in time?" Finley asked.

"I bet if you put your mind to it, you can discover how to do anything," Albert said. "To raise new questions, new possibilities, to regard old problems from a new angle, requires creative imagination and marks real advance in science. Logic will get you from A to B. Imagination will take you everywhere."

About Albert Einstein

Albert Einstein, the most famous scientist of the 20th century, was born March 14, 1879, in Ulm, Germany. He was intensely curious as a child, and wanted from a young age to understand the mysteries of science. He took piano and violin lessons, and enjoyed music as a child and as an adult.

When he was about five years old, his father gave him a compass to play with. He was fascinated with it. As an adult, Einstein wrote about this experience: "I can still remember ... that this experience made a deep and lasting impression on me. Something deeply hidden had to be behind things."

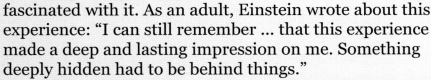

Albert graduated from the Swiss Federal Polytechnic School in Switzerland in 1900. He trained to be a physics and math teacher, but because he often cut classes to study on his own, some of his professors did not look kindly on him. After graduation, he wanted to teach at a university, but couldn't get the recommendations he needed.

In 1905, Albert finished his doctorate degree and published four papers in one of the best known physics journals at the time. One of them detailed his special theory of relativity.

Another contained his now famous formula: $E = mc^2$. This formula states that matter can be converted into energy. E stands for energy, m for mass, and c for the speed of the light in a vacuum.

Many people called 1905 Albert Einstein's "Miracle Year."

Albert developed his general theory of relativity between 1907 and 1915. It was this theory that was proven by a team of astronomers observing a solar eclipse in May 1919. Once the findings from the eclipse were published, Albert became a celebrity. Newspapers around the world published headlines celebrating his theory that redefined gravity.

Though it's not what he is most famous for, Albert was awarded the Nobel Prize in 1921 for his discovery of the law of the photoelectric effect, which says that many metals emit electrons when light shines on them.

Albert was visiting the United States when Adolf Hitler came to power in Germany in 1933. Since he was Jewish, he did not go back to Germany, where at the time he was working as a professor at the Berlin Academy of Sciences. He became a professor at Princeton University in New Jersey in 1933. He became a United States citizen in 1940 and retired from his position at Princeton in 1945. He died April 18, 1955, in Princeton, New Jersey.

In the story, Albert tells Fiona and Finley, "To raise new questions, new possibilities, to regard old problems from a new angle, requires creative imagination and marks real advance in science. Logic will get you from A to B. Imagination will take you everywhere." This is a combination of two famous Albert Einstein quotes.

Comprehension Questions

1. How did Albert Einstein change the way we understand gravity?

2. Why did it take an eclipse to prove his general theory of relativity?

3. What is special about the speed of light?

Vocabulary

inertia (i-NUR-shuh): the resistance of any physical object to any change in its state of motion

mass (mas): a measurement of how much matter is in an object

Websites to Visit

http://easyscienceforkids.com/
    all-about-albert-einstein

www.coolkidfacts.com/albert-einstein-for-kids

www.worldsciencefestival.com/2014/06/
    10-fun-albert-einstein-facts

Q & A with Reese Everett

What was the most interesting thing you learned while researching this book?
I always enjoy finding the story behind the story. Everyone knows Albert Einstein was a famous, brilliant scientist, but how did he become that person? The story about the compass his father gave him really intrigued me. You never know what will spark someone's curiosity. In this case, that simple compass was a starting point for a career that shaped humankind's understanding of the way the universe works.

Why did you make Albert Einstein Fiona and Finley's great-great-great uncle?
I didn't really mean to; sometimes things like that happen when you're writing. When I first drafted the story, I felt like Fiona and Finley's mom already knew him somehow. It wasn't until I wrote the final chapter that it occurred to me they were related, which explains a little bit why the Time Hop Sweets Shop works. Albert didn't give away the full mystery of how it works, but he did let the siblings in on their mom's secret: she's done her share of time-hopping, too!

About the Author

Reese Everett is a writer and mother of four who wishes she could time hop. She enjoys writing for young people because it gives her the opportunity to learn something new every day. When she's not writing, she's usually watching her kids play sports, or trying to talk them into an adventure. The beach is her favorite place in the world.

About the Illustrator

Sally Anne Garland was born in Hereford England and moved to the Highlands of Scotland at the age of three. She studied Illustration at Edinburgh College of Art before moving to Glasgow where she now lives with her partner and young son.